The Cats' Party

A Picture Book
by
Gerta Melle
Text by Rainer Redies

BARRON'S

Woodbury, New York / Toronto

This is the house where the cats live. Everyone here is terribly excited because Uncle Arthur and Aunt Agatha are coming to visit today with their three new kittens. The little kittens are just six weeks old, and this will be their first outing.

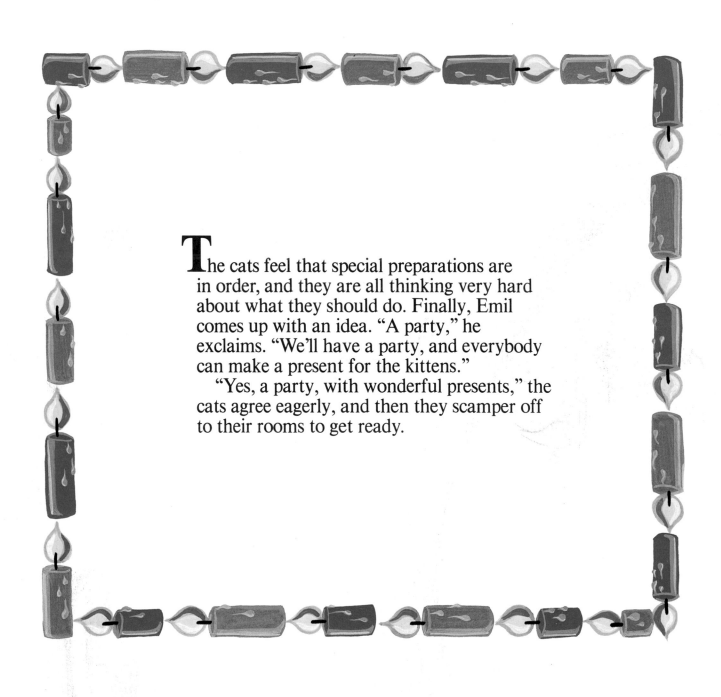

The cats feel that special preparations are in order, and they are all thinking very hard about what they should do. Finally, Emil comes up with an idea. "A party," he exclaims. "We'll have a party, and everybody can make a present for the kittens."

"Yes, a party, with wonderful presents," the cats agree eagerly, and then they scamper off to their rooms to get ready.

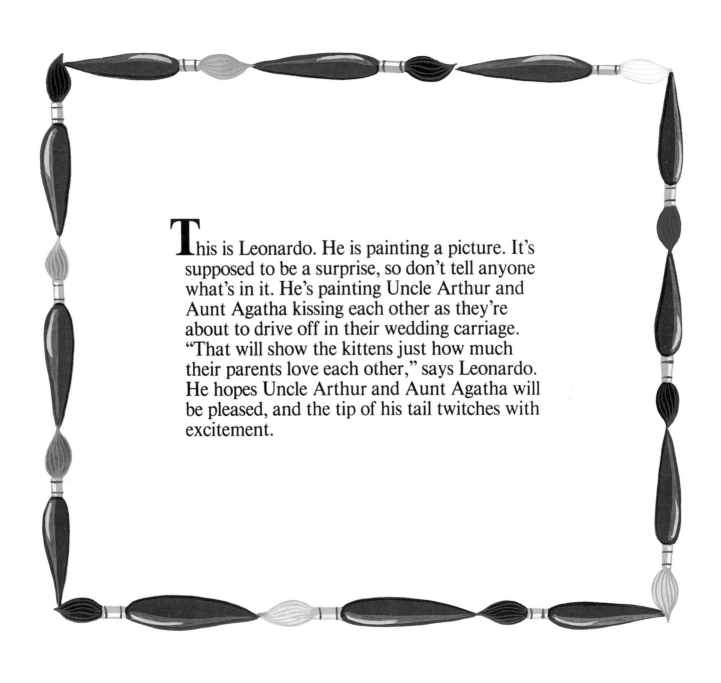

This is Leonardo. He is painting a picture. It's supposed to be a surprise, so don't tell anyone what's in it. He's painting Uncle Arthur and Aunt Agatha kissing each other as they're about to drive off in their wedding carriage. "That will show the kittens just how much their parents love each other," says Leonardo. He hopes Uncle Arthur and Aunt Agatha will be pleased, and the tip of his tail twitches with excitement.

Paul is the cook in the house. He keeps his recipes
a secret, but the kittens will love every
mouthful their uncle prepares because he
knows what kittens like best. First on the
menu will be a fish soup with all the bones
removed and with lots of heavy cream. Then
will come ham cut in deliciously thin slices.
"But the kittens mustn't eat too much," says
Paul, "or they won't have any room left for
my beautiful ice-cream cake."

Little Julie has fallen in love right up to her pretty, tufted ears. She spends her nights roaming the roof gables in the bright moonlight with her Romeo. That's why she sleeps all day. Shhh! Don't disturb her. She is dreaming sweet dreams. Tonight she will tell the kittens her loveliest dream. "Children like dreams," she says. "Dreams are food for their imaginations."

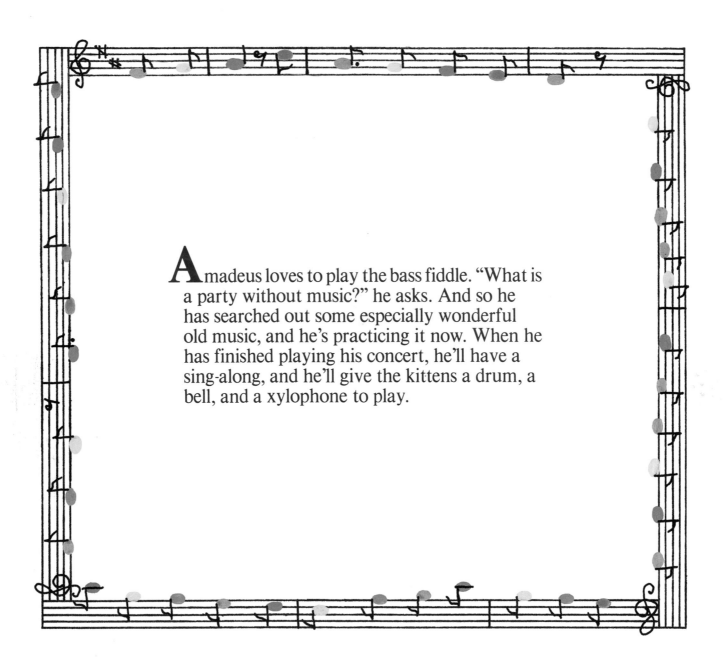

Amadeus loves to play the bass fiddle. "What is a party without music?" he asks. And so he has searched out some especially wonderful old music, and he's practicing it now. When he has finished playing his concert, he'll have a sing-along, and he'll give the kittens a drum, a bell, and a xylophone to play.

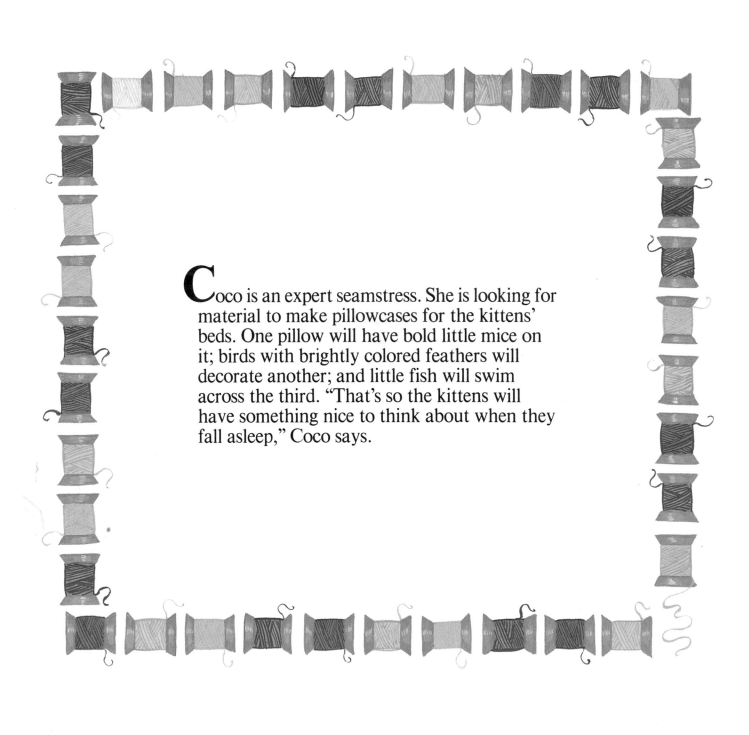

Coco is an expert seamstress. She is looking for material to make pillowcases for the kittens' beds. One pillow will have bold little mice on it; birds with brightly colored feathers will decorate another; and little fish will swim across the third. "That's so the kittens will have something nice to think about when they fall asleep," Coco says.

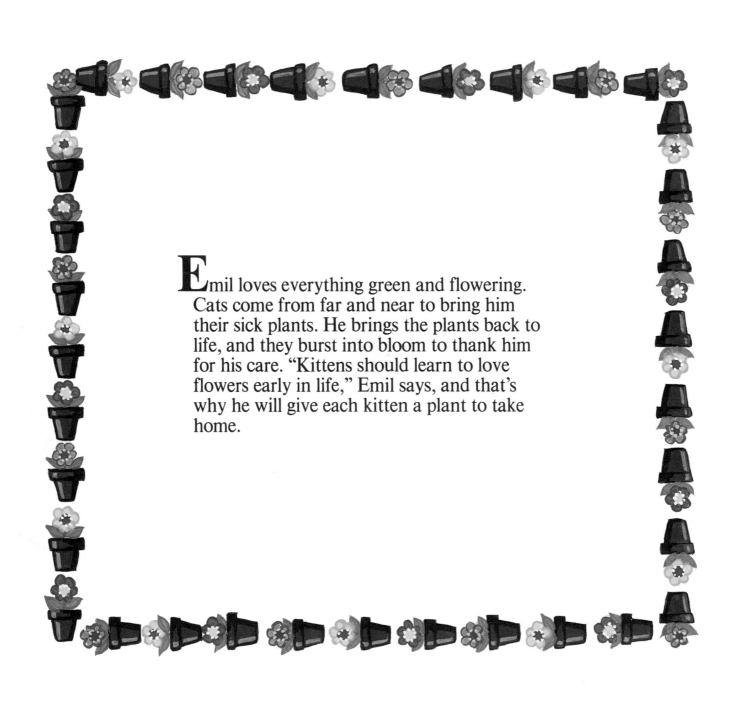

Emil loves everything green and flowering.
Cats come from far and near to bring him
their sick plants. He brings the plants back to
life, and they burst into bloom to thank him
for his care. "Kittens should learn to love
flowers early in life," Emil says, and that's
why he will give each kitten a plant to take
home.

This is Frederica writing a poem. She's been looking forward to just such a party as this for a long time. "Children enjoy rhymes," she says proudly. Now she'll have a chance to use all the wonderful rhyming words she has collected from her reading: paws and claws and guffaws and squaws, and squeeze and fleas and cheese, and chomp and romp and stomp, and scratch and catch, and cat and mouse, and fat and spouse. . . .

Whenever anything in the house is broken, Edison fixes it. But a real handyman gets tired of just repairing things, and Edison is pleased that he can now make a brand-new toy. He's going to build a car with three steering wheels, three brake handles, and three seats. Each kitten will get a seat that matches the color of its fur.

"That way there won't be any fights over who sits where," Edison says.

Everything is ready! Even little Julie has
finished her dream in time, and the guests will
be arriving any minute now. No one has
breathed a word about the many lovely
surprises that are waiting for the kittens.

"Hello, here we are!" Uncle Arthur shouts from a long way off, waving both arms. Now that their journey is over, the kittens are playing about with renewed energy. The little tom cat rushes ahead to be the first one into the house, but his sisters are close on his heels. Aunt Agatha has taken Uncle Arthur's arm. Her fur is shiny as silk, and you can tell just by looking at her how happy she is.

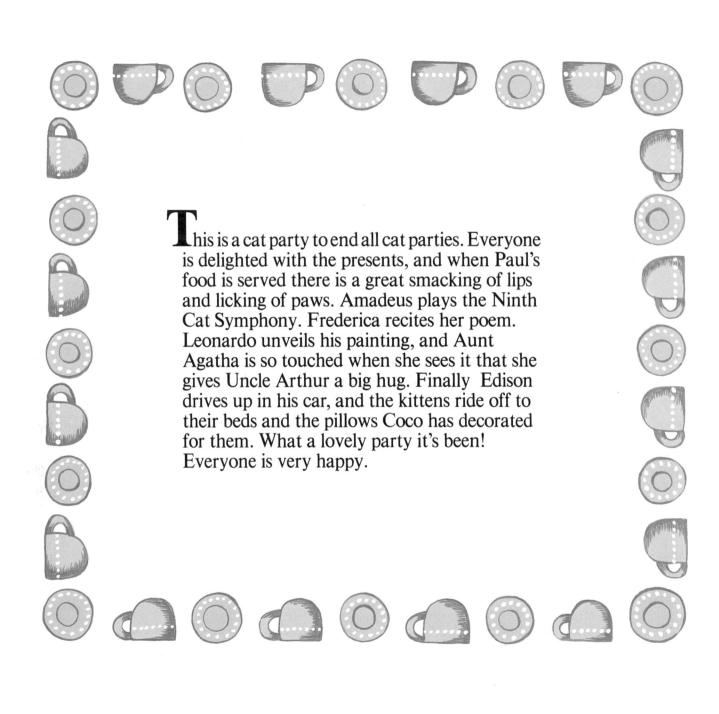

This is a cat party to end all cat parties. Everyone is delighted with the presents, and when Paul's food is served there is a great smacking of lips and licking of paws. Amadeus plays the Ninth Cat Symphony. Frederica recites her poem. Leonardo unveils his painting, and Aunt Agatha is so touched when she sees it that she gives Uncle Arthur a big hug. Finally Edison drives up in his car, and the kittens ride off to their beds and the pillows Coco has decorated for them. What a lovely party it's been! Everyone is very happy.

First English language edition in the United States and Canada
1985 by Barron's Educational Series, Inc.

Copyright © 1985 K. Thienemanns Verlag Stuttgart
Translated by Rita and Robert Kimber

First published in West Germany in 1985 by K. Thienemanns Verlag Stuttgart under
the title *Das Katzenhaus*.

All inquiries should be addressed to:
BARRON'S EDUCATIONAL SERIES, INC.
113 Crossways Park Drive
Woodbury, NY 11797

Library of Congress Catalog Card No. 85-15676
International Standard Book No. 0-8120-5720-1

Printed in West Germany
12345   987654321